ETHEREAL

A COLLECTION OF SHORT STORIES

VEERAL YASHUPAL

I dedicate this book to all those out there, who work for the development and the betterment of Humanity.

Contents

Acknowledgements *vii*

1. Endless Trigger (part I) 1
2. Endless Trigger (part Ii) 6
3. The Chamber 10
4. T Minus Two Minutes 16
5. Hawking's Party 21
6. Street 25
7. Simulated Suicide 31

Trivia 35

Acknowledgements

I'd like to acknowledge everyone who has contributed to the successful completion of this book, be it my family or my friends. Their suggestions range from macroscopic issues with the stories to tiny imperfections in grammar and detail. I thank all of them for their help and support, I owe them a major debt of gratitude.

A Special thanks to:

Varsha Suresh

Aneesh Shastri – Editor

Himani Ananth – Cover Designer

Neil Jonathan Paul – Technical Supporter

for their assistance throughout. Their dedication and effort for the betterment of the book has made this book possible. I will always be grateful to them.

I've also been substantially benefited by the feedback given by some of my friends who have read the stories. I wholeheartedly thank them.

I would love to hear from you too. Yes, you are free to provide any kind of suggestions and feedback about the book. If you just mail it to bookethereal@hotmail.com, it would greatly help.

CHAPTER ONE

Endless Trigger (Part I)

I hustled down the street to discern which star had fallen, for the crowd had gathered only to find him being interviewed. I hate it... I HATE IT when he gets the attention of the public. Nevertheless, his invention was worth it, a holographic projector, a projector that can do everything any smart electronic device can, holographically. It was better than my last invention, the AVR, a multi augmented and virtual reality device, which had attracted much less attention.

I stuffed my way through the crowd and towards Millan and I eventually reached him. We made brief eye contact but behaved as though none of us noticed the other. I must work harder. I cannot leave Millan to prove me inferior. He's a better inventor, If I cannot get to his level of ingenuity, I can bring him down to mine. If I cannot push my inventions to match his, I can bring his inventions down. This is it; his lab would be under my eye from now. I gave a roguish look to Millan and made myself scarce.

Weeks passed; It seemed like Millan had put his work to a halt. I spied his lab for days finding no trace of his next invention. I better not waste my time like this, I can invent my own piece of technology with the precious hours of the day I'm spending here. Millan is not proceeding with his work anyway.

I returned to my lab that evening and grabbed a graph paper and a pencil from the bundle to plan the blueprint of my next machinery. I had come up with an idea of an analog clock that would run on the power of magnetic induction. I came up with this when I was concerned about the time just behind Millan's lab keeping an eye on him through his broken window.

Even though no one uses an analog watch today, it could be constructed as a clock tower at the center of the city making it a tourist attraction that will surely escalate my fame. But as the state law goes, something that will be a monumental piece on the grounds of government land must undergo a demonstration proving itself to be harmless in any way to the people and the environment. Well, that shouldn't be of any concern for me... what harm can an analog clock tower running with magnetic induction power cause? I jotted down the design of the watchtower and was all set to begin with the construction. There was no prototype needed as there wouldn't be another of this kind.

Months passed; I was finally ready with the clock tower and my application to undertake the demonstration was accepted. I could not wait any longer and invited the officials near the Harmor music store at the center of the city. A large crowd had gathered, this was the moment. There was a good amount of security, and a jammer was set up to avoid any malicious activities. Regardless, I shouldn't mess up. I saw the four well-dressed women glaring at the tower, each of them being from different departments, to examine the invention. I cleared my throat, took a deep breath, and grabbed the attention of everyone, especially that of the officials by exclaiming "Good Evening, respected officials, ladies, and gentlemen!"

I went on "What you are seeing right now, is an analog clock. What's the big deal? Well, it isn't any analog clock, there's only one of this kind. It runs on the power of magnetic induction making it the only clock to depend on magnets for its energy. This, my people, will not only ornament our city but will also ensure that our state remains superior when it comes to ingenuity and architecture." A brief yet noticeable moment of applause and appreciation followed. A soft voice from the officials said "Elaborate the working."

"I sure will ma'am" I replied with a kind smile and turned to the tower.

The tower was about a hundred feet tall, the body made of concrete painted completely in wood brown with the watch at the top. The numberings on the watch were in roman numerals and the needles were black and sleek. All the internal machinery lied just behind the face of the clock.

I took out my blueprints to describe the clock's internal mecha--

"Kapow! Pow!!" I heard the gunshots followed by a large explosion. There was a bomb rigged in the tower, and the gunshot just triggered it. There was panic among the crowd, rage amongst the officials, and a great lack of certainty within me. I just then saw Millan in his winter coat with his hands in his pocket trying to hide the gun. He gave an arrogant look and sneered as he disappeared with the crowd. "Your invention is a failure Mr. Chais!!" yelled one of the officials, "For the safety of the people, the government hereby orders the tower to be demolished within an hour."

Everyone in the crowd ran away with panic. Nobody heeded the gunshot for it was barely noticeable compared to the explosion. Everyone, including the officials, strongly believed it was the clock's malfunction. Only I knew that this was Millan's plot, however, no one would believe me if I told them so. I left the clock tower there to be demolished and made my way back to my lab.

What if the bullet was aimed at me? No, the aim was clearly pointed at the clock. But a person who can shoot my invention today can also shoot my head tomorrow. A person who can plot the destruction of my creation today can also plot my assassination tomorrow. I'm now sure his ultimate aim is to shoot me to death. I'm not letting that happen, I kill him before he does. Of course, I wouldn't just show up guns-blazing to shoot him, it will be better that I wait until he tries to kill me and when that happens, I'll kill him first. From now on, I'll be spying on him much more closely.

I entered my lab, switched on the lights, and was enraged to see Millan seated on the chair. "Sad to hear about your loss, Chais." he uttered sarcastically.

"You've targeted my invention first, but I'll target you first!" I exclaimed with a frightening tone.

"Ha... Best of luck with that mate!" He replied and departed.

On my toes, I followed Millan to his lab. He went in, grabbed a sheet of graph paper and a pencil, sat down to plan something I wasn't sure of. I presumed he was planning his next invention until I saw the graph paper he held was already filled, and there was a long structure just behind him that had a grayish metallic look. He knew it! He knew that I was spying on his lab all along! He did not reveal his invention until I stopped to invent the watch. He did spy on me all along due to which, he could destroy my clock the right way, at the right time.

As for the device behind Millan, that was a never seen one. There were letters engraved at the top which I pinched my eyes to read,

'Dimension Shifter'.

CHAPTER TWO

Endless Trigger (Part II)

It took me a split second to completely comprehend and literally understand the phrase 'Dimension Shifter'. As a result of the shock, I stepped back on a black cat's tail which was in the arms of Morpheus. The cat cried in pain but, that wasn't for long, In the next instance, it moved towards an upside-down laid cardboard box, yawning and dozing off as I saw it. Millan was alerted, he came up to the window and balancing himself on his toes, tried to peek out to learn the cause of the yell.

"Schrodinger's cat!" he exclaimed after not being able to get a look at the cat as the broken window was just too high up for him.

I had, by now, hidden in the narrow passage between two residential buildings where Millan's eyes couldn't roll. Millan left; I followed suit. Millan was building the dimension shifter to change his dimension and carefully kill all of my versions there which in turn will result in my death in all dimensions. Stopping him is a must; either by not letting him go or by killing him before he does. I'll take this opportunity to do so. Destroying his machine isn't an option as he guards his machine more than the government guards Area 51.

Days pass, as I watch him make improvements to the machine by hammering, welding, and cutting it. Also, advancing the software program by frequently changing the notebook's trackpad. I wondered how he planned to assassinate me. Was it with a dagger? Nah... that'd be way violent for someone like Millan to do it. Push me off a cliff? Welp, that's another dimension, I doubt if cliffs really will remain cliffs, or if they even exist in higher dimensions. Gun? Yes, a Gun, the easiest way and he already possessed one, a pistol it was.

The next night surprisingly Millan tears the paper he almost always had in hand and gets into the machine cocking the gun he possessed. He stands inside, turns the knob-like thing, whispers "It's time to save myself" and disappears. I rushed to my lab and brought my gun with a handful of shells. I slid into his lab which was so quiet I could hear my heart pounding. Wasting no time I rushed inside the shifter, standing there, I turned towards the red knob which I saw Millan turning in a clockwise manner. There were labellings around the knob and the pointer of the knob was towards a specific one. With the fear of Millan shooting me I just pressed the knob as hard as I could.

In the next instance, it seemed like I was going up with the machine or everything else around me was going down. All of it faded as I was driven to a room that seemed the same no matter in which direction or angle you look at it. I saw Millan right above me pointing a gun at me who was just above him. For unknown reasons, this felt weird, it seemed as though I was seeing Millan in front of me even though he was above and stretching my hands straight forward even though I was raising and pointing it at Millan.

"Drop the gun dolt!" I yelled with a warning tone. Millan looking at me stammered "I- wait... how... is... how did you get here?"

"The Dimension shifter didn't forbid me from using it."

"My finger pulls the trigger you die!"

"Your finger only pulls the trigger if I don't right now--"

I saw a person just below me who seemed like standing behind me appearing from nowhere. It was Millan... It was Millan! He pointed his gun at me and I emphasized the fact that I'm pointing the gun at him above too, by looking up and stiffening my hands. Just then, another person appeared below Millan, below me. It was me there. That Chais yelled with a warning tone "Drop the gun dolt!" and the Millan below me stammered "I- wait... how... is... how did you get here?"

The same conversation goes on that went on between me and the Millan above seconds ago.

"I was just trying to protect myself from being shot by you!" cried the Millan above.

"Yeah sure, that is the reason you point a gun at me above."

"I am doing that because you have pointed the gun at me above you there"

"I- what!?" I said leaning to broaden my view.

As I looked further and beyond, I saw Millan above me pointing a gun at me above him, where I above him am in turn pointing a gun at Millan above. This just... just went on forever. More Millan and Chais appeared from nowhere below me ending up in the same situation and sharing the same startled expressions. We were stuck in a loop. There was no point of origin for this, none of us were here to kill the other first.

Millan built the Shifter as a result of his own fear of death as his conscience said I was going to assassinate him and he could save himself by killing me before I do that in another dimension. In every possible dimension, this sequence of events takes place and we all end up here. But we had reached the point of no return, none of us would agree to let the other live.

Is this where our selfishness would have led us all along? Nearly an infinite number of dimensions, and in every single one of them, we were filled with jealousy and envy, we never learned to appreciate each other, we never learnt to agree. This truly is a miserable end.

The Millan above me pulled the trigger as he heard me pulling the trigger above him, I followed by pulling the trigger of the pistol I had, for the first time putting it into action, it was unending, we were all stuck here doomed to kill ourselves over and over again. In our competition, in our spite against each other, in our greed to be the better inventor... we brought upon ourselves one of the worst fates reality can offer. As the Millan below me heard me pulling the trigger, he--

CHAPTER THREE

THE CHAMBER

"Wow! But how does it work, Maya?" I asked. Maya, a dedicated quantum physicist, a remarkable inventor, and my childhood friend had just introduced me to her new invention. She said that it was a teleportation device. I didn't quite want to get into the details of that, but I did want to understand it's working.

"Well, first of all, this is a very complex system that would take me the whole week if I start. So, it's better I just stick on to the basics and give you a glimpse of how it works," I nodded as I didn't want the science of it fleshed out either. Just a brief summary of it would be ample for me. "As you can see there are two chambers. There is a set of particles- neutrons, protons, and electrons, placed in this first chamber and another in the second chamber, there." She said pointing towards the cylindrical chambers. They were eight feet in height, and 4 feet in width, enough to fit one person at the very least.

"Basically, the particles in each chamber are somewhat bound by nature and can interact with each other. But that's not a big deal, is it?"

"No, it isn't. Even magnets are connected by the magnetic field when they are close enough."

"That's the point! These particles are linked in such a way that they remain connected no matter how far you separate them from each other.

They can interact with each other even if they are on the opposite ends of the universe. This strange property enables us to transport information between the particles. This phenomenon is known as quantum entanglement. This invention can extract information from a human body, transfer those details to its entangled chamber and the second chamber will project the information to the real world creating the same human in the first chamber. It's cool, isn't it? I might even win a Noble Prize in physics for this invention!"

I was unable to believe my ears. I would never be late to lectures again! Just step in one of the chambers with the other chamber in my class, wait till all of the science is done and there I am, in my lecture room! As far as I'm concerned, this is the best invention to date. Not only does it come with several personal benefits, but can also escalate the world economy, this would work to cut great costs and save a lot of time when it comes to transportation of goods, this will surely make our lives much better.

I was as high as a kite to use the teleporter. "What good day will it be available to the public?" I questioned Maya.

"I have just invented it. I don't even know whether it operates as intended. I have only tested this on lifeless objects. I will first test this device on living objects on the upcoming Thursday, and you can join in for the experiment if you would like to. As for the official demonstration, it will be held two weeks from now if my invention functions as intended with no issues."

"Two days later then, See you on Thursday, goodbye Maya." I said, bidding farewell.

Even though science isn't appealing to me, its inventions surely are, whose inventions are technology, or at least that's what Maya told me. Teleporters, Time machines, Quantum Computers, and what not!

I was sure that Maya's invention wouldn't have any flaw, yet my conscience questioned me "Would the new person in the second chamber be the same person?" I just wanted to be positive with my thoughts. I solaced my inner voice by saying "Of course, it will... it should!"

None of Maya's other invention have ever failed, to such a degree that it's just a waste of time making prototypes since her inventions are almost always perfect.

Despite being in a state of agitation, I behaved as though I couldn't care less about this. My mind was in a state of instability after that question. I didn't know whether to be excited or anxious for Thursday. I'd rather just keep a mindset of hope and live on a prayer till the day after tomorrow. On my way back, I stumbled upon an electronic store that had its televisions switched on. A cringy Plastic Bottle commercial was playing.

"If you empty a plastic bottle after drinking, crush and destroy it. If you really want more water, just buy a new one..."

"Hmm, now that I think about it, the working of the machine is similar to the plastic bottle, The person enters the chamber as the person's atoms are observed and then that information is transferred to the second chamber, which constructs all aspects of the person back, the physical shape, the memories, and even the consciousness, wait, can the chamber even detect consciousness, was this consciousness nothing more than the arrangement of atoms?" I felt anxiety taking hold of me, but by the time I could give it more thought, I reached my room and went straight to bed. I was too tired to think any further.

The next day just flew by after some afternoon movie, evening football, and dinner. But today, Thursday, was a big day! I was already late! I ran to Maya's laboratory like I never had before to find only Maya there. "Happy Morning Maya!"

"Good morning! Had you been any late, you would have missed this."

"Well, when the Teleporter comes to the market, this won't happen anymore," I said chuckling. Maya smiled, but I doubted if it was a sarcastic one. She continued to do her work. I wasn't sure what it was, but something with the machine. I was surprised to see no one in the lab. "Where is the person who's going to test the teleporter?"

"Who are you talking about? When did I say a person would be coming to test the teleporter?"

I thought for a moment... if no one would be coming, then who would test the machine? "Well, I'm afraid I don't understand, then who's testing it?" I asked.

"Of course," she said pointing her fingers towards herself "Who else? I invented this device; it is only fair that I test it myself."

"What! No, why are you risking your life for the sake of the success of this machine? Can't you first test it on some animal instead?"

"What kind of risk are you talking about? This is just a machine. Only a person who's not confident with his work would use timid animals!"

I didn't want to express my fear to her. It would seem as though I was doubting her invention. I just refrained from telling her anything further. There is no reason to tell her, I'm sure my fears are of just shallow concern and nothing else. The list of Maya's successful inventions is quite long, and I'm sure this will soon be another device on that list.

"Now, the teleporter is all set for the test. The only thing you have to do is just wait and watch. We'll be creating history in the field of technology today!"

There was no stopping her now. After taking a deep breath and with a smile on her face, she went into the first chamber and thumbed a blue button on the inner part of the chamber. The chamber let out a blue light which seemed to scan Maya from the topmost strand of protein to the bottom-most cell of her body. In the next instance, Maya was no longer in the first chamber. A brief, yet noticeable moment of pause followed. "Maya... are you there? Maya?" I rushed to the second chamber to find her there. I left a big sigh of relief. Nothing went wrong. "Maya, it worked!"

Maya had just received the fruits of her hard work. "You've done it!" There was no reply from her. She gazed at me with literally no expression on her face. I could see her blinking and breathing, but it felt as though she was just a mere statue. "Maya, are you okay?" There was no response.

She looked as though she was in a state of coma.

Maybe consciousness was something more than the arrangement of particles, maybe consciousness was the one thing the chamber simply couldn't scan. Maybe, the Real Maya is dead.

I waved in front of her eyes to bring her back to this world assuming she was building castles in the air after her success, but it turned out I was wrong. She just didn't respond, she couldn't.

My fear was proved right, the person in front of me was not Maya. She was just an identical copy of her, Maya was lost.

Maya was destroyed in the first chamber. Her biological replica, a mere shell with no consciousness of its own was standing before me. It's not a physical body or our appearance that makes us what we are. It is something that makes us feel that we are a part of the bigger world. The thing that controls our laugh, cry, scream and dream, everything we do. That something is what makes us, that's what we are.

We are more than just a bunch of particles arranged together, we can't just re-build ourselves by putting atoms together.

Having no idea how to react to the present situation, I stood helpless, gaping at... **The Chamber.**

CHAPTER FOUR

T Minus Two Minutes

"Reporting from OV-27 to base, confirmation for launch."

"From base to OV-27, lift-off in T minus two minutes."

"Roger that!"

Said my fellow cosmonaut Kvyat seated right beside me. The clock read 13:40 hours. The atmosphere inside the space shuttle was tense. It should be so, for we were on a mission to set the first foot of humankind on Mars. Veritably, it was only Kvyat who would step on the surface of the red planet. All I had to do was stay inside the shuttle, study the atmosphere and the presence of life on the planet while also ensuring the safety of Kvyat outside. Kvyat's face showed no sign of nervousness. He has always been that way - calm and steady. He can make the right decision even in times of emergency. He does panic a bit, but--

"From base to OV-27, lift-off in T minus forty-five seconds."

My stomach was in knots. Kvyat was rummaging through the documents in the handbag as though he was probing for something of great importance. "What is it, comrade?" I asked.

"Where's the payload info document? Never mind, just buckle up now."

I was not sure of the reason behind his concern for the payload document. With twenty seconds to spare, I didn't give a crap to his question and was more concerned about the launch.

All the necessary engines other than the main one were ignited, with the shuttle functioning perfectly normal. The radio started the final countdown -

"Three... two... one... and lift-off...! OV-27 is on its way to Mars!"

We were strapped on our seats to begin a new age of humanity. My job during the journey was easier than that of an elevator operator, I just had to keep an eye on the speed of the shuttle and the radar, making sure that nothing went wrong. I was doing my work unerringly, and everything looked ideal. We were already ninety kilometres above the ground just 10 kilometres away from the Kármán line, the frontier between Earth and Space.

"Speed status?" Queried Kvyat.

"Forty thousand kilometres per hour, comrade, good going!"

We were all buckled up in our seats while carrying out our duties in the spacecraft, we were currently experiencing an acceleration of 1.4g, which isn't a lot but even a little more acceleration than normal is enough to cause imbalance on the body. Of course, we were all trained for this and so everything was going smoothly. That is until we heard a rumble in the higher part of the ship. There was no chance of any turbulence at such a great height.

"What in the world was that?" Asked Kvyat.

"I have no idea, that's abrupt."

"From OV-27 to base, reporting unanticipated rumble." Uttered Kvyat on the radio.

There was no response. Maybe our message had reached them and they are taking the action required or... did it? Kvyat endeavored again -

"Base come in! Reporting unanticipated rumble!" No response.

This time we were certain that we had lost our connection with the base. Panic began to spread among us, I could feel my blood curdling and even Kvyat was on the verge of losing his mind.

"Speed status, speed status!" Yelled Kvyat.

"Hun... Hundred and seventy thousand kilometres per hour!"

Kvyat grabbed the radio and cried "From OV-27 to base Mayday! Mayday! Mayday! Reporting over-speeding!" The Ship was accelerating at a ridiculous rate. Everything outside the ship looked like beams of light going against us. Moreover, the trembling of the ship dominated our fear. The Fear of death. Soon, the ship should have reached a jaw-dropping speed. But the speed display... showed no reading! Nor did the digital clock! I couldn't feel myself. My weight, body, emotions, and my existence as a whole couldn't be sensed. But my consciousness was right with me. I could think and perceive but not sense touch, smell, and taste. Kvyat right beside me was fading away. I was losing his picture, voice, presence, and quiddity.

I just didn't feel weightless. It was something beyond it. A sense of derealization. A feeling of everything happening is a dream. It didn't feel like the ship was just accelerating, at least not accelerating in just 3-dimensional space. The ship continued to move until eventually, I was driven into nothingness. Sheer nothingness.

For a moment, I felt that this was the afterlife till I saw myself and Kvyat in the spacecraft trying to reach the base. I was seeing myself, but how is that even possible? Soon after that, each event of my entire life was Infront of me as some sort of a film tape. From my birth to my death, every instance of it. It seemed like all the events of my life were separated by a distance of space and not time. All of the events were taking place now, at this very moment, or at least ' this very moment ' as I see it and they will always do. I was in no state of time or place. At this instance, past, present, future, distance, and space made no sense to me. I wasn't controlling my body directly like I always do, but I just had to think about where I wanted to move and where I would be, and lo and behold, that is where I am.

I was still uncertain of what exactly was happening with me but I did know that I was looking at my life externally as an observer. I could see every moment of it, the events which have already happened, and all the events that were yet to take place, everything from my birth to my death. I did not gaze upon my future as I didn't want to live awaiting every moment. But I did, as a result of my curiosity, see where I was before my birth and where I would be after my death. I foraged for it, to find absolute nothingness. The space before the instance of my birth and after my death was blank. Is that a void yet to be filled or does it even exist in the first place? Before I could go any further with this thought, all the events around me began to distort and eventually ended up within me.

Instantly, I was given a flashback of everything that happened just after the launch and me ending up here until I opened my eyes to find myself inside the space shuttle beside Kvyat. I could feel my body. I was seemingly back into a human body, my own body. It was my consciousness, my soul, it was only ME until now. Not any physical body.

Had I been in a time slip? Even though I was uncertain of the happenings, I did realize something. Or rather, I learnt it. My life is just every moment between my birth and death. Moments that will not wait for anything. I didn't want to go into the void after my death unhappy and sorrowful. Each of the events before my death was my life. I don't know how long I'm going to live it, but I will certainly live every moment of it.

"Reporting from OV-27 to base, confirmation for launch.

From base to OV-27, lift-off in T minus two minutes.

Roger that!"

Said my fellow cosmonaut Kvyat seated right beside me. The clock read 13:40 hours. What just happened? Did it just happen, or was it yet to happen? Was this all a dream, or was nothing else real?

CHAPTER FIVE

HAWKING'S PARTY

Student's Orientation Program
On 11th July, 2304
From 10 a.m. to 1 p.m.
At Piper Auditorium, Harvard University
All the Freshman Students from all departments in the University Campus are cordially invited to attend the program. For any queries, please contact Maylor, head of the Physics and Astronomy Department.

I read the notice board of the campus. Only then did I realize the reason my inbox was spammed with the same question - "Isn't the Piper Auditorium closed due to all the mess inside?" It indeed was a mess. Due to the earthquake four days ago, which had a reading of just 3.5 on the Richter scale, the documents placed on the central table were all over the place, most of them being important ones regarding the original historical documents based on research of Sir Festin Karcz proving Einstein's theory to be superfluous and designing the first fully functioning practical time machine. The prototype was placed in an underground bunker just below the Auditorium. This was the prominent reason the Auditorium was closed. I replied to the mails saying -

Dear User,

The Piper Auditorium was closed for the time being due to the aftermath of the earthquake 4 days ago but the staff has taken care of it and the Auditorium will be open before the program.

Thanks,

William Maylor,

Head of the Physics and Astronomy Department.

It felt special to be one of the only handful of people who have access to the machine. But we were should never for various reasons. We were only allowed to touch the machine and study it providing ideas to improvise it.

After cleaning the Auditorium and collecting the papers to form a single bundle, I was called in order to segregate each one of them and place them in their right places. It was a ton of work, but something I liked as I could just take a look at all the celebrated papers in history. I started by picking the last one first, for no reason and it was Sidharath Rathore's work on teleportation which was left incomplete.

As I went on, it took me 6 hours to review and separate each one. It was already dark; the last time I remember looking at the window it was a busy afternoon street. I didn't want to do this anymore realizing that when specialty is found in abundance, it's no better than being ordinary. The next paper I picked up felt really old, it read -

You are cordially invited
to a reception for
Time Travellers.
Hosted by
Professor Stephen Hawkings
To be held at
The University of Cambridge
Gonville & Caius college

Trinity Street
Cambridge
Location - 52° 12' 21'' N, 0° 7' 4.7" E
Time: 12:00 UT 06/28/2009
No RSVP required.

Wait, Stephen Hawking? I don't remember learning about him. But an invitation for time travelers, an invitation for me! I thought over it twice, using the machine to get there did seem like a good idea and was necessary. I pushed the table and pulled the hard metallic door going downstairs. The lights switched on and stood in front of me, the huge, black L-shaped electronic gadget that had a huge input display. I rushed to that and input the data from the invitation. As far as my knowledge goes, this was all that was to be done. Just a moment later I found myself in an antique palace in front of a huge room with the sign board saying - "Welcome Time Travellers" just below it was seated a person on a wheelchair with a weird smile and the left shoulder lifted up.

His face looked as though he had played a role in the establishment of something big, something extra-ordinary. Filled with enthusiasm I was about to get out of the machine but, my inner voice stopped me. I realized, Sir Karcz designed the time machine only because of his dedication and the will to. If the past realizes that time travel will be possible in the future, they would take it pre-determined and will never look forward in inventing the machine resulting in detrimental effects. It was for the best to let time as it goes.

I finished reviewing and segregating the papers. The next day, the auditorium was all set for the program. I went out by the cafeteria as Akira, one of my students came near me with her notebook in hand.

"Professor, did you know that a scientist named Stephen Hawking hosted a party for time travelers, but no one attended."

"No, really?" I spoke.

***

CHAPTER SIX

STREET

"Past, present, future. It's just like saying 'zero plus one, one, two minus one,' it is the same thing. All of the happenings are now. Time is now, all the events we've experienced and will ever experience, and events which we won't experience, all are happening all the time. It's just that--" I was distracted in my train of thoughts by the yell of my ever-annoying Grammar teacher. "Please stand up and tell me what's a Passive voice?" He asked.

"Um... Pas... Passive voice...? Yes, it's... uh...--"

"And you were counting stars when the Sun is overhead?"

The bookworms on the front seats laughed as though these were the words that would've made even the most heartless psychopath dissolve in laughter. The Bell rang, and he couldn't yell anymore. I packed my stuff and ran out of the class as a trapped leopard would run from its now unlocked cage.

On my way back, I passed by the usual innovative mall, the backyard of the mayor's house, and The City Center Restaurant. The only thing I found unusual today, the weirdly distorted painting on the wall just behind the mall on the street. The walls of the street were not recently constructed; however, I did not recognize the painting being on the wall. I didn't bother about it as I do all the time but that image of the weird wall painting was unforgettable.

I reached my room, threw my bag on the sofa, grabbed a can of coke from the freezer, and sat down on the couch gazing at the machine I had been working on for about four years. It was a piece of machinery that could take me anywhere in time.

Yes, it was a Time Machine. I do know this sounds like a vain effort from a sci-fi fan but no, this was a real thing! But everything in my life had a problem, and this was no exception. The final and the most important thing for the machine - breaking the arrow of time via an Einstein-Rosen bridge which will be open for a short while to travel and another short while for the return journey. I had finished the work of the machine's external parts in the first year but for the last 3 years, I was just working on finding a way to create an Einstein-Rosen bridge on will, since creating an Einstein-Rosen bridge requires a ludicrous amount of energy and even a thorium-liquid Fluoride reactor would not suffice. I had to find the most precise and easiest way to create the bridge thereby reducing the energy required. This, however, is much easier said than done. I have tried tens of methods, none of them showed any signs of success.

Naturally, I was frustrated and today was no exception. To keep my thoughts away from this, I went out late at night to that uncanny wall painting. I sat on the chair which was right in front of it. I gazed at the painting wondering, "What could the eerie painting possibly signify?" After a while when the street was deserted, I saw something ghastly. The painting on the wall changed its position. Again, the painting began to move a moment later, but this time everything in my surroundings joined it. Each thing circled me accelerating every second.

Finally, everything came to a halt. But now, the painting which had nothing in it picturized a clock. A clock whose needle moved. Yes! The needle of the clock moved anticlockwise. Unnatural still, I saw a man approximately my age. He also resembled me, no, no! He was me! At least that's how it felt like. He looked around as though he had never seen a street. He moved his steps slowly but eventually reached me.

"What time is it?" he asked.

"I have no idea it might be half past midnight."

He chuckled a bit and asked, "I mean what year is it?"

"Um.... it's 2026!" I said doubting my response.

I had no idea of what was going on. A sudden movement of the painting, and then a man who looked like my twin brother appears from nowhere and asks me what year is it. At the time, I was certain that I was hallucinating as a result of overworking.

"You are getting the whole idea of the time machine wrong! You don't have to instantaneously create an Einstein-Rosen bridge. You have to make a time machine for a single planned journey, not an unplanned one. Try to gradually build the bridge, slowly bending the spacetime till the Einstein-Rosen bridge could be opened with the limited amount of energy you can provide in an instant" I was shocked by his utterances. Firstly, his solution could solve the whole problem of the machine, and secondly, how'd he know about it? I didn't utter the words 'Time Machine' even to myself in front of the mirror. "You're wondering how I know of it, aren't you?" I was dumbfounded "Look it is hard to comprehend but the truth is, I am you. I am you from the future. I just came here using the time machine you are working on." These words made my senses blur.

"You're losing your senses now. I'm not predicting your thoughts; I know it before you even think anything given the fact, I was you a year back. Oh, apologies! 1 year back I say, it's now. Whatever is taking place with you has happened to me and whatever has been taking place with me will surely happen to you shortly. I was in your shoes 12 months back leering just like you at myself from the future."

My mind was not in a position to fathom what was going on. I had not yet completed building the last bits and pieces of the machine and how did he use it to come here? He said he was from the future. Does that mean I'm travelling through time in the future? Am I coming back to this time? I was baffled by these thoughts. He went on, "This is a continuous phenomenon of time. I was told how to build the time machine when I was in your place, now I am telling you. Not a soul knows how it began and will ever know how it'll all end. This is a loop. It repeats forever, to infinity."

"So, if the future is predetermined then all of the choices in my life are not choices at all?"

"The choices of your life have already been made young man.

We are but puppets in the hands of the universe, and all our strings are pulled without the slightest mistake. However, you still have to live to understand the reasons behind your choices. The painting behaved bizarrely because of the act of disobeying the law of time, this is where the Einstein-Rosen bridge opens into. Reality is something way beyond. Something that's hidden from us; I'm sorry did I say hidden? Reality is not hidden, it's right before us, but we are nowhere near capable enough to understand it, I hope that changes sometime in the 'future'."

Saying this, he disappeared from where he appeared, nowhere. I was in utmost surety now that this was the weirdest dream I've ever had. But moments later, I realized this was not the weirdest dream, this was not a dream at all, I never slept nor did I have the habit of daydreaming. Back in my room, I applied what I told myself, at least what I from the future told myself. It took a lot of work before winding everything up. After a year of hard work and pondering, I made it.

Eureka! I had invented a Time Machine! I had to travel back in time when I was in that deserted street at night that got me to the state I am today. So, I set the location of the Einstein-Rosen bridge to that bizarre painting. And the machine began constructing the bridge. It took about two weeks for the bridge to be in a condition to open, and when it did, I took a step inside the Einstein-Rosen bridge.

What I saw in the bridge, was incomprehensible, if that painting was bizarre, this was several orders of magnitude beyond it, I would not even try to explain it as I hadn't comprehended the scene myself. And after a bit of time, well at least whatever I perceived as 'time' in the bridge, I reached my destination, I was now a time traveller, and in front of me was my younger self, seated on the chair, just as shocked as I remember.

I asked him the time, "I have no idea it might be half past midnight." He answered. I chuckled a bit, it was, in fact, a quarter past midnight, and then I asked him the year. He said what I had said back then. I told him exactly what I had told myself, making this the exact situation I was in 12 months back.

".... sometime in the 'future'" I said and went back through the bridge again came back to my time.

The time which was my present.

Past, present, future. It's just like saying 'zero plus one, two minus one, and one,' it is the same thing. All of the happenings are now. Time is now. The past, present, future, all are set in stone. The world is a puppet show and we're just puppets tied by the strings of reality. We may not have any free will, but at least we know that no matter what, we will always play our role to perfection.

***

CHAPTER SEVEN

SIMULATED SUICIDE

Simulation runs.

I was scrolling through my inbox piled up with junk. It was easier to find a needle in a haystack than a mail that is of any actual concern in this dump yard. A total of 857 e-mails were unread, most of them being ads of every single commercial brand in existence, I suppose. Scrolling through, I stumbled upon a quirky mail. What was quirky about it? Well, everything... literally. It neither had any information of the sender nor did it have any data about the time or date. The message was as bizarre as the mail looked. It read -

Dear Gras,

My identity does not matter. What matters is the reason I'm writing to you; your life is in danger in the future. It is the year 2037 and you are on the verge of death. It has nothing to do with your health. Your torso will be shot with a Luger Pistol. There is only one way you can save yourself. Here is the code to the time machine, input the following as the coordinates to the place where you will be assassinated:

40.75889676234 - 73.985130456 - 6.3710456023432 - 13.823241432234.

Purchase a pistol yourself and kill the person you find there before he does.

Thanks,

.

One of the stupidest trolls I've ever read...? Whoever it might be, the person made it feel real. I copied the so-called 'coordinates of the place I will be assassinated in the future' and clicked on the attachment the person referred to as the program to the time machine expecting a 'Never Gonna Give You Up'. It turns out he did learn a bit of programming as I clicked on it, the trackpad and mouse of my notebook became dormant and the screen asked me to input the coordinates, I pasted the combination of numbers I had copied from the mail.

No sooner had I finished submitting the coordinates than I was pulled into an incomprehensible place. It seemed like I was in a hypersphere even though I couldn't directly perceive it, it was doom-shaped at all angles as I looked around. With a lot going on, it felt like I was in the database of all the events that have taken place, are taking place, and will ever take place.

In the next instance, I found myself in front of a weapon shop. I looked around but could barely make out the place. How, what, when, where, why? How was this even possible? The store looked like it was selling stuff illegally. I couldn't question anything now, could I? This was indeed real; I purchased a pistol and a dozen of ammo as said which the keeper recommended would be the best, cheap, and easy to use. She called it a tongue-twisting L-word pistol. Maybe the problem lied in her pronunciation.

The street I was in looked very busy with old, abandoned apartments behind the stores which lodged mosses and lichens indicating the area I was in was a moist one. The street was just too crowded for even a rat to make it to the other side. I looked odd, maybe it was the way I had dressed being the only one wearing a $1/4^{th}$ short and a sleeveless while others had a semi-formal attire.

As I was trying to comprehend what really was happening, I heard a loud gunshot which echoed thrice until the origin of it was clear. It was from the sundeck of the apartment just behind the weapon shop I had purchased the gun from. No one seemed to care about it though. I lifted my head to take a look at the terrace and a person with a pistol stood on the edge. The person's face wasn't clear due to the bright moonlight behind.

Without a second thought, I rushed upstairs to the deck with my gun tightly gripped. I kicked the rusted gate to open it and closed it after I entered for the sake of safety. I pointed the gun at the person, who I recognized as a man who was also wearing different clothes than the others on the street.

"Hey!" I called out to him. As he turned to realize that I was pointing the gun at his abdomen, he was petrified, yet he quickly curbed his fear and cried -

"No wai--" Before he could complete, I pulled the trigger. It shot right through his liver. He fell off the deck, as I walked to the edge to take a look at his fall. Surprisingly, he was nowhere to be found..., neither was there any trace of his fall nor did the crowd go around losing their nerves due to the sound of the gunshot. I tried to clear my mind and analyze the situation, The person I shot, his face, someone I've seen before, and he was wearing a..., WEARING A $1/4^{TH}$ SHORT AND A SLEEVELESS. Then I heard it:

"Hey!"

I turned to find a person WEARING A 1/4TH SHORT AND A SLEEVELESS pointing the gun at me. It was me killing myself all along! A Bootstrap Paradox! Before he could pull the trigger, I cried

"No wai--". I was shot. Yet, I wasn't bleeding, I couldn't feel any pain, no, I couldn't feel anything. Thinking with what sanity I had left, I found myself falling through a void with the moonshine gleaming on me, I saw myself fading away into the void, it was, Ethereal. If only I had thought this through. If only I took the time to realize what was going on. If only I hadn't acted on impulse. Farewell.

Simulation stops.

"The simulation is beautiful; the storyline is breathtaking." Said a voice.

"Indeed, the simulation of this 'human' civilization in the Milky Way is quite amusing, we never programmed their destruction. Thankfully, we found out that event needs no code. They were created to be their own destroyers."

The supernatural beings chuckled.

Trivia

Endless Trigger

- When Millan exclaims "Schrodinger's Cat!" in Part II, it serves as a joke as he is not able to take a look at the cat, therefore, he has no idea if the cat exists, or doesn't. It both exists and doesn't at the same time based on the principle of Superposition, hence, Schrodinger's cat.
- This story takes inspiration from the Many worlds theory in Quantum mechanics, where there will be basically infinite number of universes encapsulating every single possibility of every single event. Of course, in that case, the Plot of the story would not have happened in every single universe, but a small portion of infinity, is still infinity. So, the plot remains accurate in that particular case.

The Chamber

- Quantum Entanglement is a property. Teleportation as a whole is a real-world phenomenon and has already been done in the scale of particles. It is unsafe and just no better than impossible do it on a macroscopic scale as it takes a lot of time to scan each and every particle from a body, teleporting it and recreating the body.
- In this story, we have interpreted consciousness as something more than just the arrangement of particles

or the pattern of neuron impulses, something beyond what we perceive, something Ethereal. Of course, this will probably not be the case in the real world, but we suppose we'll just have to see, after all, we know very little about the concept of consciousness.

T Minus Two Minutes

- Kvyat's concern about the payload documents hints about the malfunctioning of the flight, it could be said that there were some 'dangerous cargos' in the payload which caused this event. Since it takes place decades in the future, it would be safe to assume our technology would have gone far enough to facilitate the events in the story.
- The void the narrator finds himself in can be considered a viewpoint in higher dimensions, perhaps the events in the story led the narrator to travel beyond the 3-dimensional view point we usually live in.

Hawking's Party

- This story was based on a real event, where Dr. Stephen Hawking actually hosted a party for time travelers and only gave the invitation after the party to make sure only genuine time travelers attend the party. Of course, no one attended the party but that might be due to something similar in the story. This story might be a real possibility, and we would never know.

- Though it is highly unrealistic Harvard would use papers and pen 82 years in the future, this is explained by the fact we humans would like to preserve our history, and therefore preserve the original documents, written on paper. The notebook mentioned at the end of the story was simply a digital one.

Street

- An Einstein-Rosen bridge, popularly known as wormholes, forms the core concept of time travelling in this story. And the thorium-liquid fluoride reactor is an efficient nuclear fission reactor frequently discussed amongst nuclear physicists.
- The time machine, was approximately the size of the room, 3 quarters of the time machine was the reactor, and at the remaining part there was machinery to focus the energy into a single point thus enabling the creation of the bridge. The clock which rotates anticlockwise was just a finishing touch added by the narrator, which was present behind the opening to the bridge.

Simulated Suicide

- The coordinates mentioned in the mail (40.75889676234 - 73.985130456 - 6.3710456023432 - 13.823241432234) are actually the coordinates for Time Square, NYC, USA and the third co-ordinate is derived from the radius of the earth (6371 km). The 4th co-ordinate, the time co-ordinate is derived from the name of the universe (13.8 billion years).

- The concept of existing in a simulation, indeed ethereal... or is it? Look around you, sense and perceive each and everything you see, feel, hear, taste and smell. Close your eyes and picture the vast universe we have in our limits. Nature has been designed in a beautiful way, each and every system to be unique and efficient per se. Isn't all of this just too perfect to not be pre-programmed?

***

Printed by Libri Plureos GmbH in Hamburg,
Germany